WE
SHALL
OVERCOME

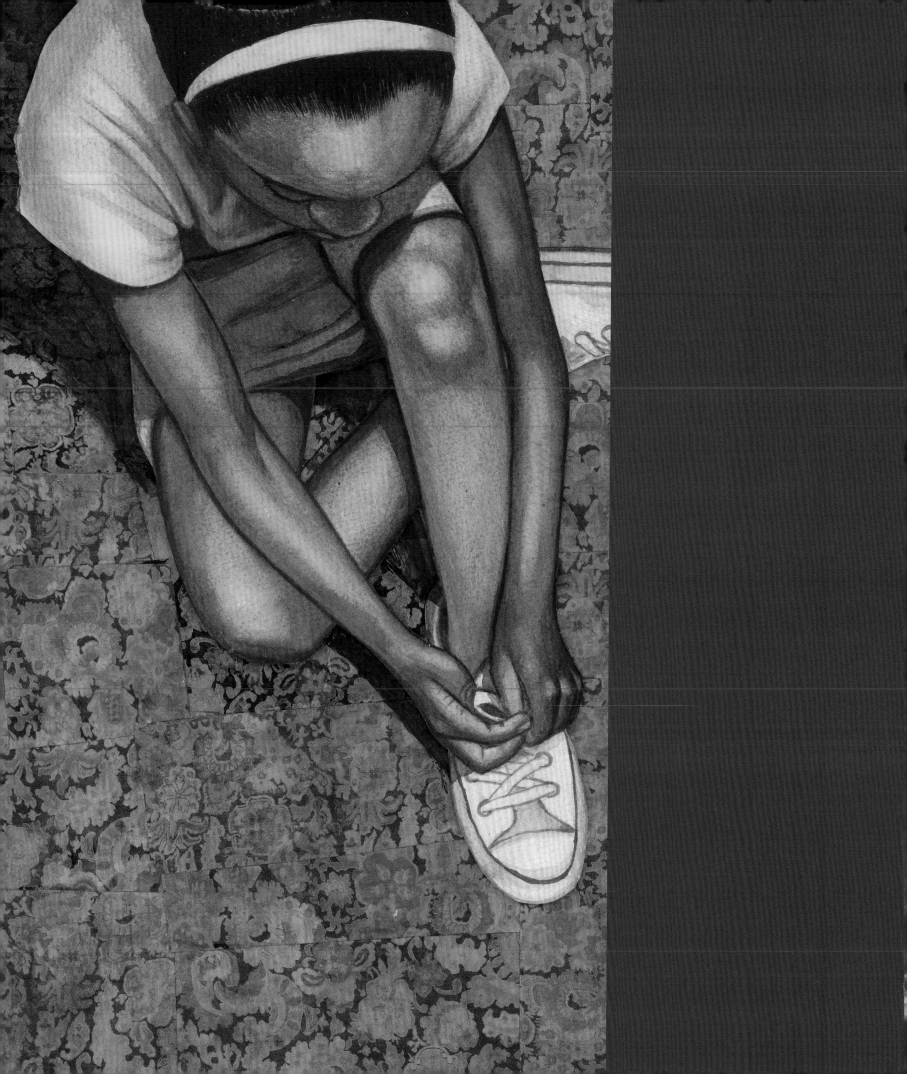

BRYAN COLLIER

WE
SHALL
OVERCOME

ORCHARD BOOKS

NEW YORK
AN IMPRINT OF SCHOLASTIC INC.

WE SHALL OVERCOME, WE SHALL OVERCOME,

WE SHALL OVERCOME SOMEDAY.

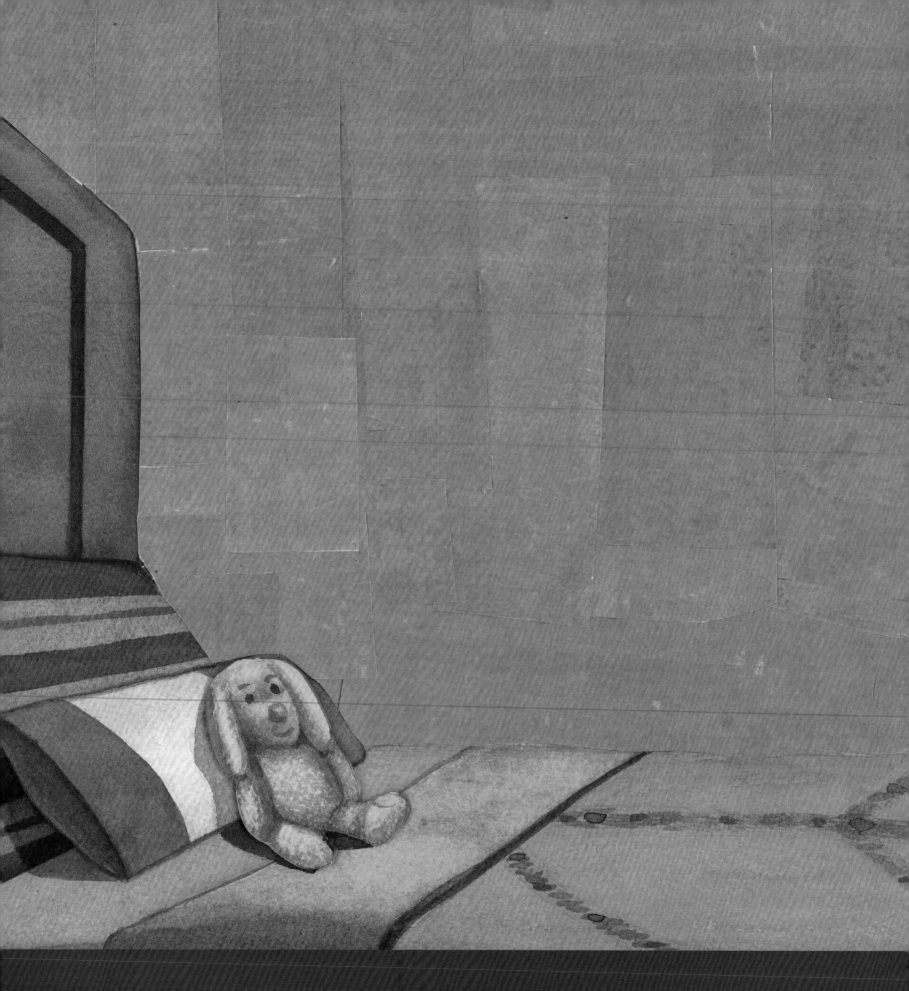

OH, DEEP IN MY HEART, I DO BELIEVE,

WE SHALL OVERCOME SOMEDAY.

THE LORD WILL SEE US THROUGH.
THE LORD WILL SEE US THROUGH.

THE LORD WILL SEE US THROUGH SOMEDAY.

OH, DEEP IN MY HEART, I DO BELIEVE,

THE LORD WILL SEE US THROUGH SOMEDAY.

WE'RE ON TO VICTORY, WE'RE ON TO VICTORY,

WE'RE ON TO VICTORY SOMEDAY.

OH, DEEP IN MY HEART, I DO BELIEVE,

WE'RE ON TO VICTORY SOMEDAY.

WE'LL WALK HAND IN HAND,
WE'LL WALK HAND IN HAND,

WE'LL WALK HAND IN HAND SOMEDAY.

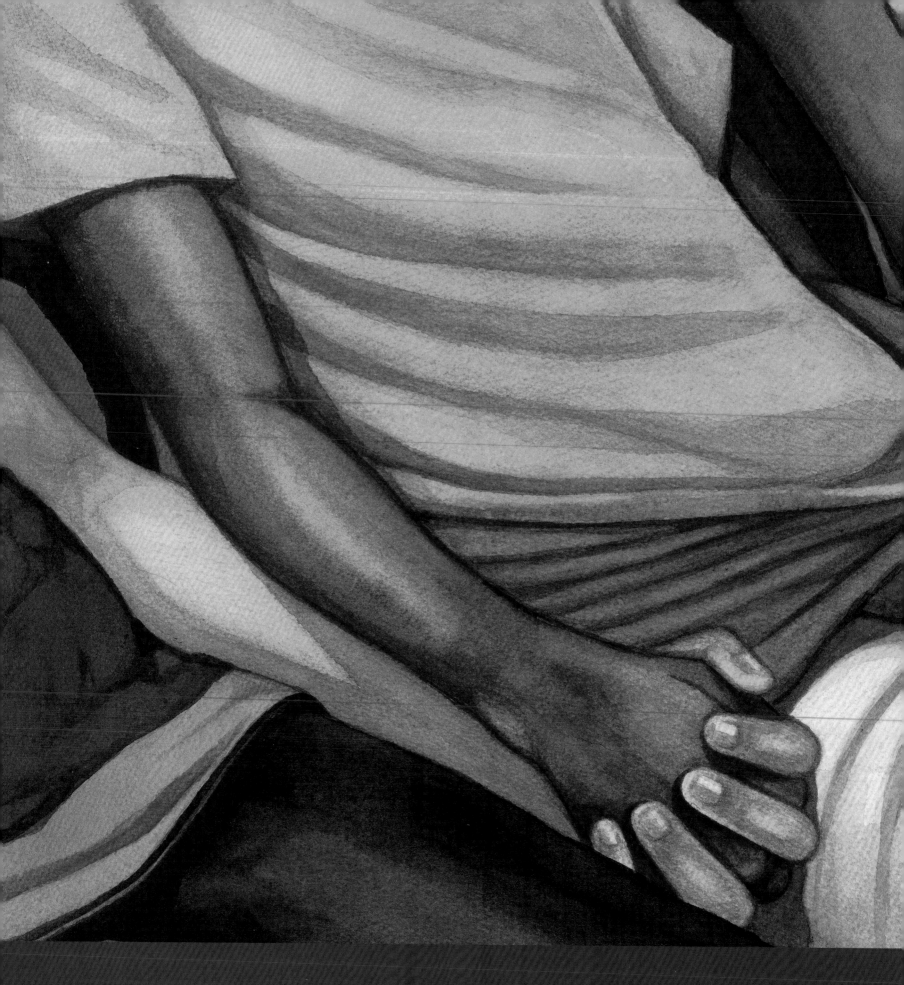

OH, DEEP IN MY HEART, I DO BELIEVE,

WE'LL WALK HAND IN HAND SOMEDAY.

WE ARE NOT AFRAID, WE ARE NOT AFRAID,

WE ARE NOT AFRAID TODAY.

OH, DEEP IN MY HEART, I DO BELIEVE,

WE ARE NOT AFRAID TODAY.

THE TRUTH SHALL MAKE US FREE,
THE TRUTH SHALL MAKE US FREE,

THE TRUTH SHALL MAKE US FREE SOMEDAY.

OH, DEEP IN MY HEART, I DO BELIEVE,

THE TRUTH SHALL MAKE US FREE SOMEDAY.

WE SHALL LIVE IN PEACE,

WE SHALL LIVE IN PEACE,

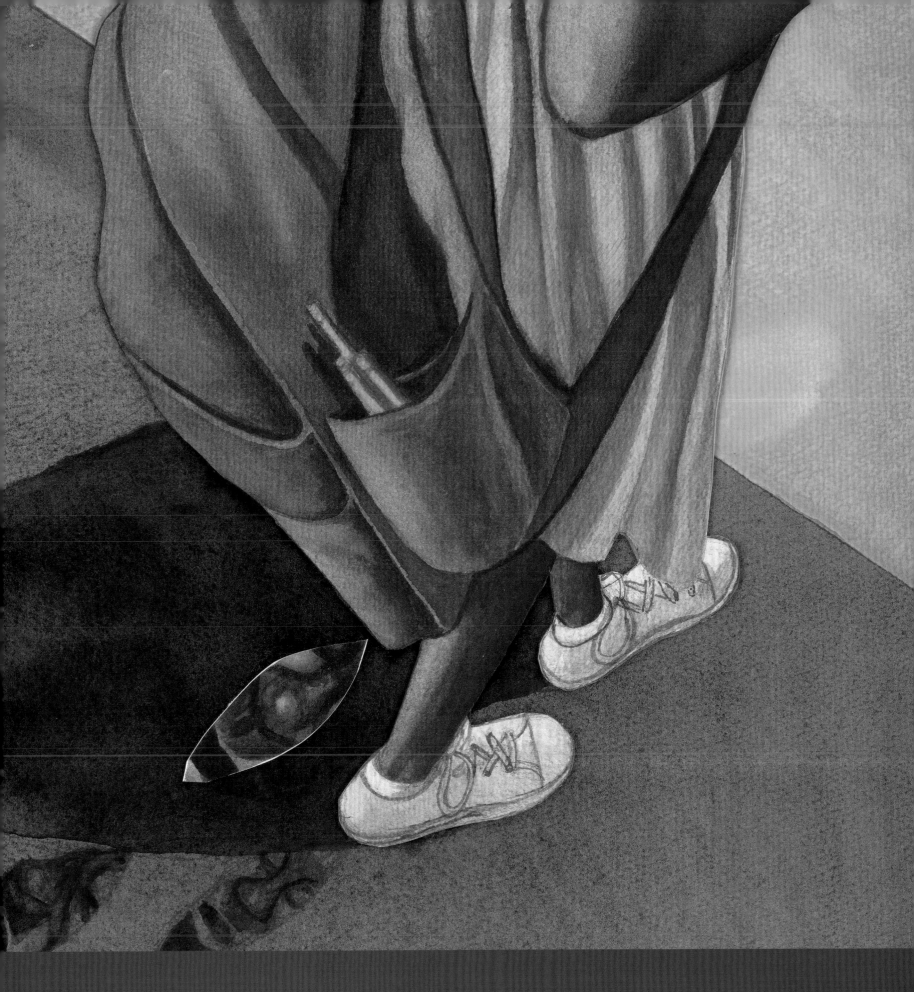

WE SHALL LIVE IN PEACE SOMEDAY.

OH, DEEP IN MY HEART,

I DO BELIEVE,

WE SHALL LIVE IN PEACE . . .

. . . SOMEDAY.

WE SHALL OVERCOME HISTORY

The original lyrics to the song that would later inspire "We Shall Overcome" as we know it today first began as a song sung by enslaved people. It then moved to hymnal books in churches, then became a cry for fair wages at union strikes, and finally moved to become an anthem for hope.

The roots of "We Shall Overcome" stretch as far back as 1900, sung by those seeking justice. Over time the lyrics have changed, the rhyme and rhythm rewritten to match the cadence of footsteps marching toward a brighter future. Pete Seeger popularized the version of the song widely known today.

During the Civil Rights Movement, the song became an anthem for freedom and change. It served as a rallying cry for peace and equality. People sang the song as they boycotted and protested, were arrested and harmed. The song never lost its power, and it continued to be a beacon of hope. Dr. Martin Luther King Jr. famously sang the lyrics in his final sermon in Memphis. It was also sung at his funeral, in remembrance of the hope he gave us all.

The tune has been sung as far away as Prague, used to give hope to protestors that one day their government would bring about change to unite their country. It has been translated from English to Hindi, Bengali, and more, proving that the idea of hope is in fact universal.

HISTORICAL MOMENTS

DID YOU NOTICE THE CHURCH ON PAGES 12 AND 13?

That is the 16th Street Baptist Church in Birmingham, Alabama. In 1963, members of the Ku Klux Klan bombed the church, which murdered four young girls and injured fourteen people who were inside preparing for a special event. The KKK bombed the church because they did not believe Black people deserved the same rights and privileges as white people. The 16th Street Baptist Church is still standing today. Directly outside the church, at Kelly Ingram Park, stands a statue of Dr. Martin Luther King Jr. The statue stands to remind us that as long as injustice exists, the fight for equality is never over.

DID YOU NOTICE THE BUS ON PAGES 14 AND 15?

That bus is a replica of the bus Rosa Parks refused to give up her seat in. In 1955, there were laws in the South called Jim Crow laws. These laws were used to continue to keep Black people from having access to and receiving the same rights and privileges as white people. These laws were often called "separate but equal," but they were never equal. On December 1, 1955, Rosa Parks sat down in a bus seat after a long day of work. As people loaded the bus, there weren't any available seats for white people to sit. The bus driver demanded that Rosa Parks give up her seat (and stand) for a white person. Rosa refused and, as a result, was removed

from the bus and arrested. Her arrest spurred the first large demonstration against segregation. The Montgomery Bus Boycott lasted a little over one year and showed the nation that Black people would not tolerate injustice.

DID YOU NOTICE THE SCHOOL ON PAGES 20 AND 21?

That is Little Rock Central High School. In 1954, the federal government declared that segregation in schools throughout the United States was unconstitutional. This meant that it was now illegal for Black and white children to learn separately. This ruling upset many white people, specifically, the governor of Arkansas, who on the first day of school, sent armed guards to Little Rock Central High School to block nine Black students from entering the school. The Little Rock Nine were nine Black students who were supposed to start school at Little Rock Central High. After days of protests and riots, President Eisenhower sent in National Guardsmen to escort the nine safely into school.

DID YOU NOTICE THE BLACK LIVES MATTER MURAL ON PAGES 32 AND 33?

Black Lives Matter is a statement and a movement. The goal of Black Lives Matter is to bring attention to the unjust treatment of Black people by the police. Black people and sometimes children are victims of police violence at a higher rate than other people. The work of the Civil Rights Movement helped pave the way for the Black Lives Matter Movement. This is why the song "We Shall Overcome" remains so important. It acts as a rallying cry for people to stand up and speak out against injustices so that there may finally be a day when we are all equal.

I dedicate this book to both the young and old with encouragement, much like my main character (the African American girl in the yellow dress), to take a walk, a stroll, or a sprint while on your journey to examine and connect the past to the present in hopes of gaining a better understanding of the future.

—B.C.

ILLUSTRATOR'S NOTE

"We Shall Overcome" is a well-known song of protest as African Americans and others marched and fought for equality during the 1950–60s Civil Rights Movement. When Reverend Charles Albert Tindley published the hymn "I'll Overcome Someday," he could have never imagined it would turn into a song with such a far-reaching impact on people seeking freedom all over the world.

Painting in watercolor and collage, I reimagined this text by incorporating historical landmarks and Civil Rights figures painted in black and white, including 16th Street Baptist Church in Birmingham, Alabama; a statue of Dr. Martin Luther King Jr.; Mrs. Rosa Parks refusing to stand, which started the 1955 bus boycott; and Little Rock Central High School in Arkansas.

Painted in full color, and depicting a contemporary young African American girl and her friends on their way to school, these scenes show just how far we've come as Black and white children march through this timeline in history, and with the freedom to walk to the same bus stop and attend the same school together. As the story progresses, I also wanted to reveal that there is more work to be done as the children march on through a Black Lives Matter mural in which I painted faces in each of the footprints, connecting the present and past, and all who marched before us.

The battle continues in the quest for justice and equality, and my hope is in the end, we may find Peace.

10 9 8 7 6 5 4 3 2 1   21 22 23 24 25 • Library of Congress Cataloging-in-Publication Data available • ISBN 978-1-338-54037-6 • First edition, November 2021 • Book design by Rae Crawford • The art for this book was created with collage and Winsor & Newton watercolor paint on 300lb. Arches watercolor paper.